SABRINA

A Great Smoky Mountains story

words and pictures by Lisa Horstman

D1402960

©2015 Lisa Horstman. Story, illustration, and design by Lisa Horstman. Edited by Steve Kemp. Project Coordi........ by Steve Kemp.
Printed in Hong Kong 2 3 4 5 6 7 8 9 10
ISBN 978-0-937207-80-2 (softcover)
ISBN 978-0-937207-81-9 (hardcover)
Published by Great Smoky Mountains Association in cooperation with the National Park Service.
P. O. Box 130, Gatlinburg, TN 37738 (865) 436-7318 www.SmokiesInformation.org
All purchases benefit the educational, historical, and scientific programs for Great Smoky Mountains National Park.

This book is for H.W. Horstman 1921-2014. You did good, Dad. —LH

Sabrina dropped...

...and dropped, until...

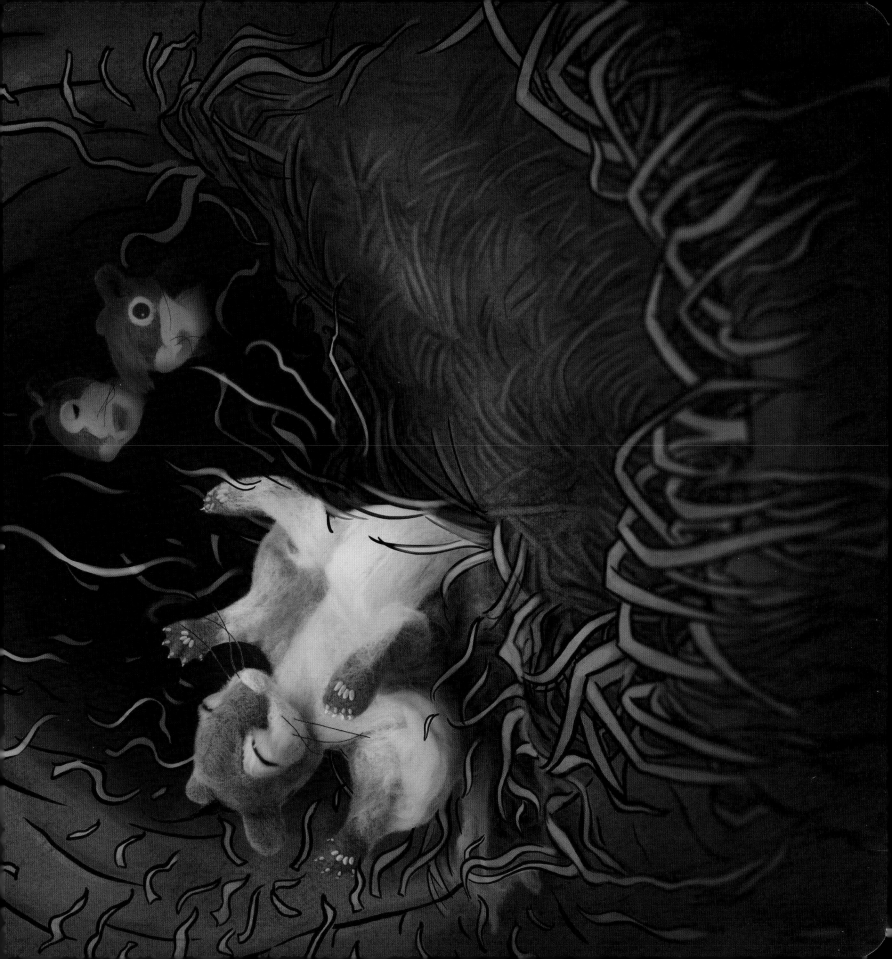

Here is
Mama Red.
Yeah, can't a
guy get any sleep
around here?
He is
Pine Nut.
That is
Chickpea.

No, Sabrina was not a red squirrel, like the others.
She was a FLYING squirrel. She just didn't know it yet.

But flying squirrels stay awake all night and sleep all day.

The next day, Sabrina was so sleepy.

Because Sabrina was so sleepy,
she was also very clumsy.

Oh, how Boomer, Pine Nut, and Chickpea chattered! (Because red squirrels don't laugh. They *chatterchatterchatter*.)

A favorite game was guessing just what Sabrina *was*.

Hey, maybe you're a *SKUNK!* Can you lift your tail and spray?

If you can do *THAT*, then I bet you're a skunk!

Sabrina was pretty sure she *wasn't* a skunk.

But most of the time,
the red squirrels ignored
Sabrina.

One night, the nest had a
very unwelcome guest.

Sabrina, as usual, was awake.

The others were not, until…

—a very *hungry* owl.

Sabrina decided to do something very, *very* brave.

The owl, who never liked to be insulted, fixed his big eyes on Sabrina.

And Sabrina jumped...

...and glided! Her arms acted as wings. Sabrina saw she could change direction by tilting and moving her tail a certain way.

"I'm a flying squirrel! But we don't really fly at all. We glide," thought Sabrina.

The owl snatched Sabrina and carried her away.

They passed a colony of bats...

...and bears sleeping
in a tall tree.

At sunrise the owl reached his
lair high up in the Smokies.
It was time for breakfast.

The owl lunged right, and Sabrina swerved left.

The owl lunged left, and Sabrina swerved right.

The frustrated owl screamed and lunged again. This time he clamped onto Sabrina's head...

...and the helmet stuck in the owl's beak! Sabrina popped her head out of the helmet.

The owl shook his head. He flapped
his wings. He stomped. But the
acorn helmet held fast in his beak.

He forgot about Sabrina, and
Sabrina dropped...

...and dropped,

and dropped.

But this time, she knew how to glide to a safe landing.

The panicky owl flapped away, never to return. (Last we heard he'd moved to Florida.)

Now Sabrina was a hero to the red squirrels. They even wore acorn helmets, just like Sabrina, in case the owl ever came back. (He didn't.)

But they were never able to glide like Sabrina.

Life went on.
The red squirrels
did red-squirrelly
things, and Sabrina
did flying-squirrelly
things.

And then, one night...

Four more things about flying squirrels:

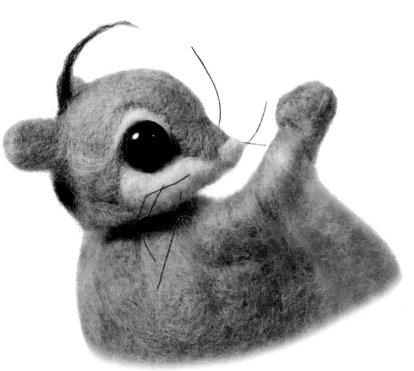

1 The loose extra skin between their wrists and ankles acts like glider wings when stretched tight.

2 Dinner tonight: nuts, mushrooms, lichens, seeds, berries, spiders, and other tasty bugs.